I'm Going To R

These levels are meant only as guides;
you and your child can best choose a book that's right.

Level 1: Kindergarten–Grade 1 . . . Ages 4–6
- word bank to highlight new words
- consistent placement of text to promote readability
- easy words and phrases
- simple sentences build to make simple stories
- art and design help new readers decode text

Level 2: Grade 1 . . . Ages 6–7
- word bank to highlight new words
- rhyming texts introduced
- more difficult words, but vocabulary is still limited
- longer sentences and longer stories
- designed for easy readability

Level 3: Grade 2 . . . Ages 7–8
- richer vocabulary of up to 200 different words
- varied sentence structure
- high-interest stories with longer plots
- designed to promote independent reading

Level 4: Grades 3 and up . . . Ages 8 and up
- richer vocabulary of more than 300 different words
- short chapters, multiple stories, or poems
- more complex plots for the newly independent reader
- emphasis on reading for meaning

LEVEL 2

2 4 6 8 10 9 7 5 3 1

Published by Sterling Publishing Co., Inc.
387 Park Avenue South, New York, NY 10016
Text © 2006 by Harriet Ziefert Inc.
Illustrations © 2006 by Emily Bolam
Distributed in Canada by Sterling Publishing
c/o Canadian Manda Group, 165 Dufferin Street,
Toronto, Ontario, Canada M6K 3H6
Distributed in the United Kingdom by GMC Distribution Services,
Castle Place, 166 High Street, Lewes, East Sussex, England BN7 1XU
Distributed in Australia by Capricorn Link (Australia) Pty. Ltd.
P.O. Box 704, Windsor, NSW 2756, Australia

I'm Going To Read is a trademark of Sterling Publishing Co., Inc.

Library of Congress Cataloging-in-Publication Data

Ziefert, Harriet.
  Fooba wooba John / Harriet Ziefert ; pictures by Emily Bolam.
    p. cm.—(I'm going to read)
  Summary: Easy words with a rhyming refrain describe the strange
antics of a variety of animals.
  ISBN-13: 978-1-4027-3420-5
  ISBN-10: 1-4027-3420-4
  [1. Animals—Fiction. 2. Stories in rhyme.] I. Bolam, Emily, ill.
  II. Title. III. Series.

PZ8.3.Z47Foo 2006
[E]—dc22   2005034433

Sterling ISBN-13: 978-1-4027-3420-5
ISBN-10: 1-4027-3420-4

For information about custom editions, special sales, premium and
corporate purchases, please contact Sterling Special Sales
Department at 800-805-5489 or specialsales@sterlingpub.com.

FOOBA WOOBA JOHN

Pictures by Emily Bolam

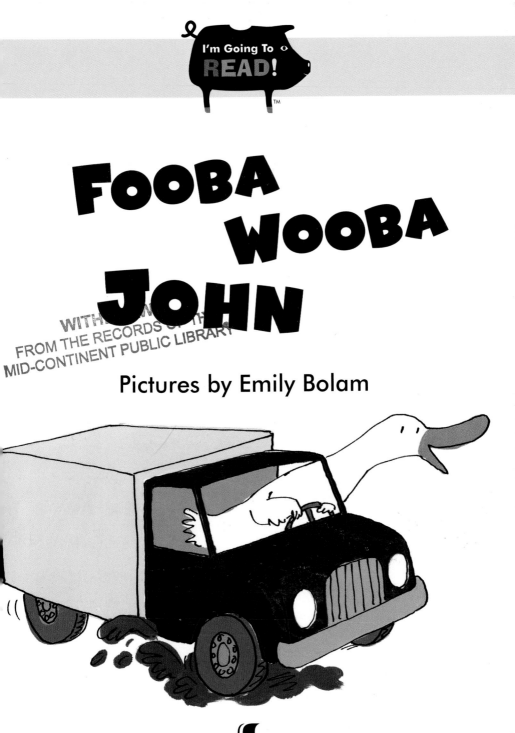

Sterling Publishing Co., Inc.
New York

Saw a flea kick a tree.
Fooba wooba,
Fooba wooba.
Saw a flea kick a tree,
Fooba wooba John.

Saw a flea kick a tree,
In the middle of the sea.
Fooba wooba,
Fooba wooba,
Fooba wooba John.

Saw a crow flying low.
Fooba wooba, fooba wooba.
Saw a crow flying low,
Fooba wooba John.

Saw a crow flying low,
Several miles beneath the snow.
Fooba wooba, fooba wooba,
Fooba wooba John.

Saw a rat wear a hat.
Fooba wooba, fooba wooba.
Saw a rat wear a hat,
Fooba wooba John.

Saw a rat wear a hat,
Sitting on a baseball bat.
Fooba wooba, fooba wooba,
Fooba wooba John.

Saw a baboon use a spoon.
Fooba wooba, fooba wooba.
Saw a baboon use a spoon,
Fooba wooba John.

Saw a baboon use a spoon,
Eating ice cream
on the moon.
Fooba wooba,
Fooba wooba,
Fooba wooba John.

Saw a moose drinking juice.
Fooba wooba, fooba wooba.

Saw a moose drinking juice,
Fooba wooba John.

Saw a moose drinking juice,
In a great big red caboose.
Fooba wooba, fooba wooba,
Fooba wooba John.

Saw a frog in a bog.
Fooba wooba, fooba wooba.

Saw a frog in a bog,
Fooba wooba John.

bog   frog

Saw a frog in a bog,
Sitting on a great big log.
Fooba wooba, fooba wooba,
Fooba wooba John.

Saw a sheep take a leap.
Fooba wooba, fooba wooba.
Saw a sheep take a leap,
Fooba wooba John.

Saw a sheep take a leap,
From a pretty purple jeep.
Fooba wooba, fooba wooba,
Fooba wooba John.

Saw a duck drive a truck.
Fooba wooba, fooba wooba.

Saw a duck drive a truck,
Fooba wooba John.

Saw a duck drive a truck,
Through a pile of mucky muck.
Fooba wooba, fooba wooba,
Fooba wooba John.

Saw baby Gus make a fuss.
Fooba wooba, fooba wooba.
Saw baby Gus make a fuss,
Fooba wooba John.

Saw baby Gus make a fuss,
Riding on a city bus.
Fooba wooba, fooba wooba,
Fooba wooba John.

Saw a sheep in a jeep.
Fooba wooba, fooba wooba.
Saw a sheep in a jeep,
Fooba wooba John.

Saw a sheep in a jeep,
Driving up a hill that's steep.
Fooba wooba, fooba wooba,
Fooba wooba John.

What did you see?